# Wild Science: Learning from the Cheetah

by Patricia Drudy

## Houghton Mifflin Harcourt™

**PHOTOGRAPHY CREDITS:** COVER (bg) ©Gail Shumway/Getty Images; 3 (b) ©Gail Shumway/Getty Images; 4 (b) ©Buena Vista Images/Getty Images; 5 (t) ©Andrew Harrington/Alamy Images; 6 (t) ©Franz Aberham/StockImage/Getty Images; 7 (t) ©Ali Jarekji/Reuters/Corbis; 8 (b) ©James Warwick/The Image Bank/Getty Images; 9 (t) ©Ben Radford/Corbis; 10 (b) ©G. Ronald Austing/Photo Researchers/Getty Images; 11 (t) Cheetah robot image courtesy of Boston Dynamics/WENN/CB2/ZOB/NewsCom; 13 (b) ©Beverly Joubert/Getty Images; 14 (b) ©Getty Images/PhotoDisc

Printed in the U.S.A.

ISBN: 978-0-544-07323-4

13 14 15 16 17 18 19 20  1083  20 19 18

4500710511          B C D E F G

# Contents

| Vocabulary | Stretch Vocabulary | |
|---|---|---|
| observation | behavior | trait |
| hypothesis | wildlife biologist | physicist |
| data | geneticist | roboticist |
| evidence | | |

# Introduction

Cheetahs captivate people with their strength and grace. These big cats fascinate scientists, too. Life scientists, such as zoologists and biologists, study cheetah behavior and genetics. Physical scientists want to know just how these animals can move so fast. Earth scientists study the effects of drought and climate change on cheetah populations. Each kind of scientist looks at the cheetah for different reasons.

Different kinds of scientists use similar methods. First, they make observations. From observations, a scientist may make a hypothesis, a possible (but not necessarily correct) answer to a question. The hypothesis is tested through an investigation. All scientists use tools to collect data, or information. The data scientists collect is evidence that will either support, or not support, their hypothesis.

Running at speeds exceeding 113 kilometers per hour (70 miles per hour), the cheetah is the fastest of all land animals.

# Observations in the Wild: Survival Challenges

The cheetah is facing a big problem. It is Africa's most endangered cat. Wildlife biologists, scientists who study wild animals and their habitats, want to protect the cheetah.

Cheetahs can live in a variety of different environments—from mountains to grasslands—but they need a large amount of land and a large number of available prey animals in order to thrive. Once, cheetahs could be found all over Africa and Asia. Today, although cheetah populations still exist in Africa, they are limited to fewer countries. Scatterings of cheetahs in Iran are all that remain of the Asian population.

Wildlife biologists have found that many factors have contributed to the cheetah's decline. A growing human population has contributed to a loss of habitat and prey. People have also hurt the cheetah's chances for survival by hunting them.

Currently there are around 10,000 cheetahs roaming the savannas and grasslands of Africa.

This cheetah is being fitted with a GPS tracking collar.

But there is hope for the cheetah. The work of wildlife biologists has led to the creation of international laws that protect the big cats. Today it is illegal to hunt cheetahs anywhere.

Wildlife biologists place GPS (Global Positioning System) tracking collars on cheetahs. A collar can send information to a computer that tells the trackers where a cheetah is located. Scientists can use the information to tell how far cheetahs travel. They can share information with other scientists and conservationists. The information can be used to set up wildlife preserves with plenty of space for the cheetah population to grow successfully.

Cheetahs share 99% of the same genes. They are as closely related as identical twins.

## Observations in the Lab: Genetic Diversity

Cheetahs are not able to fight diseases as well as other animals. Geneticists wanted to know why. A geneticist is a scientist who studies genes, microscopic parts of the body that contain DNA and are responsible for the traits of every living thing. Traits are characteristics, such as size, color, way of moving, and behaviors. Traits make one person—or, in this case, one cheetah—different from another.

Traits also include the chemicals in blood. Geneticists have studied the blood from different cheetahs. All the cheetahs they have studied have the same proteins in their blood. In most animals the proteins vary, just as other traits do. Scientists concluded that most cheetahs are as closely related as identical twins! There is not enough genetic diversity, or difference, between individual cheetahs. One outcome of this is that cheetahs are often not successful in reproducing.

Geneticists are trying to increase the genetic diversity in cheetahs. They are hoping to improve the cheetahs' ability to fight disease.

Scientists now know that cheetahs share 99% of the same genes. But what does this mean? One thing it means is that cheetahs are less successful at fighting disease than many other animals. Scientists have learned that if a virus gets into, for example, a leopard population, only some animals will die. This is because leopards do not have identical genes. But if every animal has the same genes, like the cheetah, and one gets sick, all of them may become sick. Because of their identical genes, a deadly virus could kill many more cheetahs. So, in addition to outside threats like loss of habitat and prey, the cheetah is threatened by its own genetic structure.

## Built for Speed

Why are cheetahs the fastest runners on Earth? This is a question some physicists want to answer. Physicists are physical scientists who study matter, energy, and motion. You might not think that physicists would study animals. But some physicists want to understand how the cheetah runs so fast.

Physicists use cameras and video to record images of cheetahs running. They analyze the images frame by frame. Physicists have learned that every part of a cheetah's body is made for speed. The cheetah is smaller and lighter than other big cats. It's usually less than 1 meter (3 feet) tall and 1.2 meters (4 feet) long. More than half of a cheetah's length is its tail. It turns out that the tail is key to the cheetah's control during a 113 kph (70 mph) chase. It prevents the cheetah from spinning out during fast turns!

Cheetahs use their remarkable speed to catch prey.

Like cheetahs, greyhounds are built for speed. They can achieve speeds of 68 kph (43 mph).

How are cheetahs able to achieve such quick bursts of speed? Physicists answered this question with an experiment. Cheetahs were compared with greyhounds, dogs that can run very fast and are used for racing. The scientists had both animals chase after a piece of chicken. They recorded the motion and measured the force created by each animal. They concluded from the data that cheetahs vary their strides at different speeds. At 32 kph (20 mph), the cheetahs took 2.4 strides per second. At 61 kph (38 mph), the cheetahs took 3.5 strides per second. Greyhounds run with the same stride at different speeds.

The scientists could not get the cheetahs to run any faster than the greyhounds, even though cheetahs are much faster. Why? Scientists think that the cheetahs lacked enough motivation to chase a piece of chicken at their best speed!

## Robot Cheetah

Physicists are not the only physical scientists interested in the cheetah. So are roboticists, the people who design and build robots. Robotics is a field that combines knowledge from several different physical sciences as well as from engineering. Roboticists develop robots for many reasons. Often they are trying to create robots to do repetitive or even dangerous tasks for humans. Some robots can defuse bombs. In the future, robots may be essential to deep space exploration.

A group of roboticists wanted to build a robot that moves very fast. They decided to study the cheetah's body. They used slow-motion cameras in order to observe the movement of a cheetah's spine. Cheetahs' spines bend. This makes it possible for the animal to run with long strides. Roboticists collected data showing that one cheetah stride could cover 7 meters (22 feet)! They also observed that cheetahs lift all four feet off the ground at two points in their stride.

The cheetah's spine can bend back and forth. The long strides help the animal accelerate.

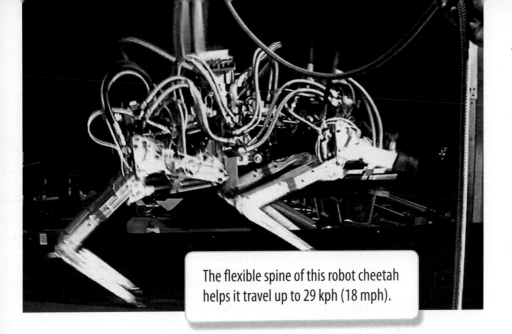

The flexible spine of this robot cheetah helps it travel up to 29 kph (18 mph).

Roboticists wanted to build a robot that had a bendable spine, like the cheetah. They built a robot cheetah with a spine that moves back and forth on each step. This lets the robot run with a long stride. The long stride helps the robot cheetah run super fast. In 2012, a version of the cheetah robot set a new speed record for robots at 29 kph (18 mph)! Although this is much slower than a cheetah, the robot's speed is much faster than the average human. An average man can only run about 24 kph (15 mph) for short periods.

Researchers are still improving the cheetah robot. They hope that one day it will run as fast as a real cheetah!

## Cheetahs and Climate

Earth scientists are also interested in the cheetah, but for very different reasons. They want to understand how climate changes may be contributing to the decline of cheetah populations. Climate is what the weather is like over a long period of time. In recent years, many areas of East Africa have been experiencing warmer temperatures and less precipitation than normal. These are the same areas where cheetahs live.

Normally, East Africa is warm most of the year. In addition, it has two rainy seasons. There is usually one rainy season from March to May that brings heavy rains. Another rainy season from October to December brings lighter rains.

In 2011, rainfall amounts in this area were far below normal. Some areas of Kenya received only 10 percent of their average annual rainfall. While this area is known for having occasional droughts, or long periods of time without rain, this drought was one of the worst in sixty years. The lack of water affects all living things in the environment, including cheetahs. Less water leads to a decline in the population of the cheetah's prey. Less water also means a decline in cheetah habitat as more land becomes barren and unlivable.

The preferred prey of cheetahs is the Thomson's gazelle. These gazelles provide cheetahs with the protein they need to maintain good health. Although these gazelles are well adapted to surviving in dry regions, long-term droughts cause their populations to decline. With a decline in the gazelle population, cheetahs are forced to prey on a variety of other animals, including rabbits and antelope. These animals do not provide as much protein for the cheetahs as gazelles do.

Why is a high-protein diet so important to the cheetahs' survival? It seems that such a diet is necessary for cheetahs to reproduce successfully. With fewer gazelles to feed on, fewer cheetah cubs are being born. Even when a cheetah mother gives birth to a normal litter of four or five cubs, the chances of even one of the cubs surviving into adulthood are slim.

A drought affects all of the living things in an area.

## The Benefits of Research

Research on cheetahs has resulted in contributions to several areas of science. Studying cheetah genes has even helped medical research. Because cheetahs have identical genes, they can receive organ transplants from other cheetahs. Most other animals reject transplants. By studying a cheetah body's reaction to a transplant, scientists may learn something that will help human patients accept transplants.

When scientists from different fields study the same animal from different perspectives, we can learn more about different aspects, or parts, of the animal. The cheetah is in danger of becoming extinct. Scientists working both in the field and in the lab may help save the cheetah.

There is much scientists can learn by studying cheetahs.

### Observe Like a Scientist

Use a variety of tools, such as a hand lens, metric ruler, and scale, to observe a small organism in your environment. You could observe a snail, an insect, or a small lizard. For example, use the hand lens to observe and make a drawing of the organism. Use the metric ruler to measure its length. Use a scale to measure its weight. Record the data in a chart, and share your work with the class. Include a sketch of the organism, with labeled parts.

### Understand Different Perspectives in Science

Work with a partner to select an animal that you both would like to learn more about. Then write three different questions: one that could be answered by a life scientist, one by an Earth scientist, and one by a physical scientist. Use the Internet to gather data that will help you come up with good questions. Then write ideas for the kinds of investigations each type of scientist might use to answer the question.

# Glossary

**behavior** [be·HAV·yur] The actions displayed by an organism in response to its environment.

**data** [DEY·tuh] Individual facts, statistics, and items of information.

**evidence** [EV·uh·duhns] Data gathered during an investigation.

**geneticist** [ge·NET·e·sist] A scientist who studies how traits are passed down between parents and offspring.

**hypothesis** [hy·PAHTH·uh·sis] A possible explanation or answer to a question; a testable statement.

**observation** [ahb·zer·VAY·shuhn] Information collected by using the five senses.

**physicist** [FI·zi·sist] A scientist who studies motion and energy.

**roboticist** [ro·BOT·e·sist] A person who designs, builds, and experiments with robots.

**trait** [TRAYT] A characteristic of a living thing.

**wildlife biologist** [WILD·life bi·OL·o·gist] A scientist who studies wild animals and their habitats. They are often involved in conservation and protection of animals.